THE
SNOW
SISTER

FABER & FABER

has published children's books since 1929. Some of our very first publications included *Old Possum's Book of Practical Cats* by T. S. Eliot, starring the now world-famous Macavity, and *The Iron Man* by Ted Hughes. Our catalogue at the time said that 'it is by reading such books that children learn the difference between the shoddy and the genuine'. We still believe in the power of reading to transform children's lives.

Emma Carroll

Illustrated by Julian de Narvaez

FABER & FABER

First published in 2015
by Faber and Faber Limited
Bloomsbury House,
74-77 Great Russel Street,
London WC1B 3DA
This edition published in 2017

Typeset by Faber and Faber
Printed in England by CPI Group (UK) Ltd, Croydon, CR0 4YY

A CIP record for this book is available from the British Library

ISBN 978-0-571-34180-1

FSC
www.fsc.org
MIX
Paper from
responsible sources
FSC® C101712

2 4 6 8 10 9 7 5 3 1

To dearest Karl,

the original Snow Sister

1

The Last Will and Testament of Silas Granger

Christmas Eve morning wasn't the best time for a telling-off, yet Pearl Granger was about to get one. She had been outside in the snow for all of two minutes, when above her head a window opened and her mother's voice rang out.

'What in heaven's name are you doing, you daft child?'

Pearl flinched. 'It isn't what it looks like, Ma.'

What it *did* look like was a girl in a patched-up frock putting the finishing touches to a person made out of snow. And that person, with two pilfered pieces of coal for eyes and a turnip for a nose, was now wearing Pearl's sister Agnes's best shawl.

'Bring that back inside this instant, do you hear?' Ma said, and Pearl knew it wasn't the coal or the turnip her mother meant, though both were in short supply. Ma shut the window again with a slam.

Pearl sniffed back her tears. She wasn't going to cry, not when it was very nearly Christmas and the snow lay so thick and beautiful on the ground. Ever since she could remember, she'd loved snow. So too had Agnes, and together they'd rolled in it, fought in it, shut their eyes and tasted it. Even without Agnes the snow still made everything seem better, like a clean sheet over an old mattress.

And Pearl was proud of her finished snow sculpture. The size of a real-life girl, it had a sharp face, a certain tilt to the head. With Agnes's shawl now in place – and with a good deal of squinting – it might almost be her sister stood before her.

Almost. But not quite.

With a sigh, Pearl removed the shawl and, holding it to her face, breathed in. Agnes's smell was of violets – the sweets, not the flowers. After she died it had lingered in the house, as if she couldn't quite leave. Only when Ma packed Agnes's things in a tin trunk did the violet smell disappear. A year later, and though it was bad luck to keep them, all their mourning clothes were folded and stored away inside the same trunk. Yet the blackness in their hearts proved more difficult to hide.

That tin trunk, Pearl knew, was kept in the cellar between the coal heap and the vegetables. Three winters it had been there. Three winters of her sister's clothes hidden away, so that instead of hand-me-downs Pearl made do with letting out skirt hems and patching up stockings worn thin at the toes.

Not that she minded. Each winter when it snowed, she crept down into the dark for two bits of coal, a turnip and something of Agnes's from the trunk to make a snow person.

Or more precisely, a snow sister.

It didn't bring her sister back. And the snow person always melted in the end. Yet for a little while she had a snow sister, which meant she missed Agnes just a tiny bit less.

Today, though, Agnes's best shawl didn't smell of violets. Pearl breathed deeper, willing

some scrap of her sister still to be there, but all she got was a nose full of dust that made her sneeze.

'Bless you!'

It was Mr Leonard, the postman.

'That hill on Heather Lane don't get any smaller,' he puffed. 'And now everyone's sending these new *Christmas* cards, I'm feeling like a pack mule!'

He stood red-faced on the path that led past six identical front doors, Pearl's being the first cottage in the row. The bag he wore strapped across his chest certainly looked fuller than usual. But Pearl's eyes went to the envelope in Mr Leonard's hand.

'Take it straight in to your pa,' the postman said, giving her the envelope. ''Tis an official letter. Postmark says it's from Bath!'

She frowned. *Bath?*

Bath was a day's walk away and full of

fine, tall houses, so Pa said. She didn't know anyone who lived in Bath, and yet she felt a dancing in the pit of her stomach and wasn't sure why.

With the letter in her hand she hesitated.

'*To Mr Barnaby Granger,*' it said.

The writing, squiggly and expensive-looking, was on an envelope so thick it might've had a whole pamphlet inside.

'Go on, hurry!' said Mr Leonard. Waving her inside, he carried on to the next cottage in the row.

Pearl took a deep breath. She felt that flutter in her stomach again. The letter was important, she was sure of it. What she didn't know was whether this was a good thing or a bad.

Inside, she found her father lacing up his work boots. Already he had his coat and hat on because with the fire burning so feebly, it wasn't any warmer here than outside. He glared at the shawl in her hand. 'You been upsetting your mother?'

She gave him the letter, tucking Agnes's shawl under her arm as she did so. 'This came. Postmark says it's from Bath.'

He sat up straight.

'Oh,' Pa said, turning the envelope over. 'Oh.'

Pearl swallowed nervously. That moment Ma stormed down the stairs.

'Pearl, you can't just go taking that shawl . . .' Seeing Pa's face, she stopped. 'Whatever is it, Barnaby?'

'We have a letter,' he said. 'From Bath.'

Ma moved closer.

Pearl wished he'd just hurry up and open it. Then everyone might forget about Agnes's shawl and she could sneak it back into the trunk without another word. But she knew Pa wouldn't be able to read the letter, not with his spectacles broken and no money for a new pair.

'Want me to read?' she offered.

Pa nodded and gave the envelope to her. Inside was just one sheet of very thick paper. The words on it were written in that same fancy, squiggly hand.

Pearl cleared her throat.

'*Dearest Sir,*' she read. '*You are requested to attend the reading of the last will and testament of Mr Silas Granger . . .*'

She glanced up.

'Silas *Granger*? Is he a relative, then?'

From the look on her parents' faces she knew he was, though she'd never heard the name before. So the letter was bad news. A will meant that someone had died; *a Granger*, she thought, and felt her tears well up again even though this person wasn't close like a sister. They hadn't died of fever, here in this very house, whilst holding tight on to her hand.

Yet Pa soon recovered himself. 'Well, well. All that money couldn't save the old devil in the end.' Then he nodded. 'Read on, Pearl.'

She took a nervous breath.

'. . . *on Thursday 24th December at Whitstone and Whitstable Solicitors, Argyle Street, Bath. Proceedings will begin at two p.m. As the main beneficiary in the document you are strongly advised to be prompt* . . .'

Looking up, she saw her parents' faces had changed. Pa was almost smiling. Ma's hand covered her mouth like she was fighting back a laugh.

'What's a beneficiary?' Pearl asked.

'It means he's left us something in his will,' said Pa.

Ma shook her head. 'Only *something*? Barnaby, you're the *main* beneficiary! Looks like he's left you the lot!'

Taking the letter from Pearl and pocketing it, Pa got to his feet. 'Bath? Today at two p.m.?' He glanced at the mantel clock. 'If I get a shift on I might make it in time.'

'But you'll lose a day's work,' said Pearl, growing confused. Though Pa was a wheelwright by trade, the work had become unreliable. People travelled more and more by train these days. There was less call for carriage wheels. And even fine, handcrafted ones like Pa made would never run as smooth as those on train tracks. So a day's work, when it came, was important.

'This is *vital*. He has to go,' said Ma. And her parents shared a look that to Pearl seemed almost feverish.

'Who exactly is *Silas Granger*?' she asked,

even more confused.

'He is . . . sorry, *was* . . . your uncle, your father's only brother,' said Ma, 'though they moved in very different worlds.'

'Why haven't I heard of him before, then?'

Her father paused. 'We never got on, not even as boys. He always wanted bigger and better. Didn't care how he got it, neither. 'Tis no surprise he got rich. We lost touch over the years.'

Ma interrupted. 'Now, Pearl, let your father get going else he'll never make it to Bath.'

'But why's he left us something if you didn't get on?' Pearl said. She couldn't imagine not caring for your own flesh and blood. Not speaking for all those years. It felt such a terribly sad waste.

'Don't you fret, girl. Chances are we're about to become rich!' said Ma.

Pearl stared at her ma, then her pa. '*Rich?*

Us?' This was getting madder by the minute!

'Perhaps our luck's changing, Pearlie-Pearl,' Pa said, chucking her under the chin. 'Now stop worrying.'

Yet still Pearl didn't know what to make of it. From the doorstep, she waved Pa off until he was nothing but a trail of dark footprints in the snow. She hoped he was right, that life was about to get better. In the meantime Ma, at least, was smiling again, and seemed to have forgotten about telling her off.

2

Christmas Pudding

No sooner had Pearl closed the door than the next surprise hit her with a wallop.

'This year we're going to have ourselves a proper Christmas feast,' said Ma, rolling up her sleeves.

Pearl blinked. What the heck was happening here today?

Since Agnes's death, they'd not made a fuss about Christmas. It was easier not to, when the sight of her sister's empty seat at the table was hard enough even on normal days.

'Are you sure?' Pearl said, for there was also the question of money. Not until Pa heard Uncle Silas's will and came home with the news would they know for certain *how* rich they were to be, if at all. In the meantime, they were stuck with a fire not hot enough to cook on, and a crust of day-old bread.

Yet Ma was now stoking the stove in a very determined fashion. 'Think on what your pa said, Pearl. When he comes home tonight, he'll bring news of our fortune. Because that's what your Uncle Silas has left us – a great fortune, I'm certain of it.'

'But how . . . ?'

Her mother spun round. 'Don't you doubt it, my girl. This is our luck changing at last, and it's time for us to start changing with it.'

Pearl felt Agnes's shawl still tucked under her arm. After three long years, her sister's smell had almost gone. Perhaps Ma had a point. Maybe things were about to change for the better, and it was time to put their grief behind them. Well, she supposed, she could try.

'A proper Christmas it is, then,' Pearl said, squaring her shoulders. 'And a proper Christmas needs a proper pudding.'

'Good girl,' said Ma. 'Now, I'll find some more coal. You go and speak nicely to Mr Noble at the grocer's.'

Which, Pearl knew, meant begging for more credit. Only this time, she hoped it would be her last.

Town was but a short walk down the lane. Yet the snow, top-of-boot deep in places, made the going slow, and Pearl thought of poor Pa on his way to Bath. She dearly hoped a passing carter would take pity and offer him a ride, otherwise he might not make it back by tonight.

By the time she reached town she was sweating, made worse by Agnes's shawl, which Ma had tied around her before she left.

''Tis time you had it, really,' Ma said.

Its red-and-gold paisley suited Pearl's dark hair well. Though without it, her snow sister back home now looked rather plain, and hardly like Agnes at all.

The main street was heaving with shoppers and sellers and carts whizzing by. Pearl squeezed her way through the crowds. But on reaching the town square, she suddenly stopped. Her mouth fell open in awe.

In the middle of the square was a fir tree decked with lights. It was easily as tall as a

door, and twice as wide. The lights, she saw now, were little fluttering candles. Snow, still falling softly, sat like fine sugar on the branches. Pearl felt certain she'd never seen such a magnificent sight.

In fact anyone walking past the tree – women, children, men in top hats – seemed to slow down and smile. Pearl guessed this *thing* they all stared at was a 'Christmas tree'. In the newspaper there had been pictures of Queen Victoria and Prince Albert next to one, except theirs had been *indoors*. She couldn't imagine such a tree inside her own tiny cottage. A person would have to live in a vast house with great, high-ceilinged rooms.

She then remembered Pa's letter from Bath.

If Pa comes home rich, maybe we'll live somewhere like that, she thought with a delicious shiver. *And next Christmas we'll have a tree indoors.*

It couldn't hurt to dream. Right now, though, she had pudding ingredients to get, and by the town clock it was already nearly half past nine.

She set off again. The next part of the main street was lined with stalls selling spiced cider and hot pies, oranges and nuts, cut glass and flowers. As the crowds slowed her pace, Pearl couldn't help but look at the lovely things for sale. Ma would like one of those little blue enamel brooches. And what about a scarf for Pa? The green was such a fine colour. But even wearing Agnes's best shawl over her patched-up clothes, the stallholders knew she couldn't afford anything.

'Don't touch that, miss,' they said, watching her like a hawk. 'It's too pricey for your sort.'

My sort, eh? thought Pearl crossly. *Maybe not for much longer!* It was on the tip of her tongue to say so too, but they'd only laugh, so in the end she gave up and walked on.

A left turn off the main street brought her at last to 'Noble & Sons, Grocer'. Either side of the door, two bay windows curved out over the pavement. Waiting opposite those windows was a carriage, its colour a distinctive ladybird-red. Pearl knew it instantly: it belonged to the Lockwoods, the richest family for miles. They weren't 'old money', Pa always said, for Mr Lockwood had made his fortune on the railways, but they certainly had plenty of it. Yet here they were shopping at Mr Noble's just like ordinary folks did. Perhaps they'd have even more in common soon, Pearl thought with a smile.

As she opened the shop door it flew suddenly inwards. Pearl went with it. Stumbling into the shop, she fell to her knees on the sawdust-covered floor.

'Good gracious! What an entrance!' said a

rich-sounding voice.

Pearl froze. Someone had been on the other side of the door. And that someone now stood over Pearl. She knew the voice all right, and she saw, at eye level, a pair of finest pale blue gloves gripping a package wrapped in paper.

'Sorry, Mrs Lockwood,' she stammered, scrambling to her feet.

The entire shop fell silent.

Mrs Lockwood tutted, then, with a sweep of her skirts, was gone. The door jangled shut behind her. The remaining customers stared at Pearl. She smiled awkwardly, brushing sawdust from her frock. When they turned back to their shopping, she sighed in relief and took her place in the queue.

Staring at the shelves stacked floor to ceiling with tins and jars, Pearl soon forgot Mrs Lockwood. In her head she rehearsed how she'd ask Mr Noble very nicely for credit. *More* credit. When it came to her turn, though, it was the shopkeeper's daughter who served her.

'Flour, please,' Pearl said. 'And sugar, and some butter. Oh, and some raisins and mixed peel.'

There were other ingredients needed too. She watched as the girl weighed things out, then wrapped them neatly in brown paper. The last time she had made a pudding was with Agnes, who'd chased her round the kitchen with baking mixture all over her hands. A sad ache filled her chest.

At last the parcels were ready.

'How're you paying?' asked the girl.

Pearl took a deep breath. 'On the account, please.'

'The name?'

'Granger.'

There was no flicker of concern, no refusal.

The girl simply nodded. Seven perfectly wrapped parcels lay on the counter; Pearl scooped them into her arms. She couldn't believe how easy it'd been. Perhaps Pa was right and their luck *was* changing.

She'd almost reached the door when Mr Noble's voice boomed behind her. 'Stop there, Miss Granger!'

She paused. Her legs went weak.

'Bring those goods back, please.'

A hush fell over the shop. Pearl felt people's eyes on her yet again. Her face grew hot. The parcels, piled up to her chin, were threatening to slide out of her grip.

Mr Noble came out from behind the counter.

'No more credit,' he said, his aproned chest puffed out. 'Not until your family's account is settled.'

A parcel of currants slid to the floor.

Next went the flour, landing with a dusty thump. Jiggling her arms, Pearl tried to catch the sugar, but that went tumbling too.

'You'll be charged for what you ruin, mind!' Mr Noble warned, making no effort to help her.

She knew she should dump what parcels she still had and leave. By now she was close to tears. It was Christmas. She'd only wanted a bit of good cheer for once. And tomorrow her family might be rich, perhaps as rich as the Lockwoods, and then they'd pay off their account tenfold. But just like those stallholders, Mr Noble wouldn't believe her if she told him.

So she didn't go to the counter. She did a flit.

3

To Catch a Thief

'Stop! Thief! Filcher!' Mr Noble cried
from his shop doorway.

Passers-by stopped dead. Babies
went quiet in their mothers' arms. Even
carters in the street tugged their reins. Quick
as she could, Pearl ducked and weaved her
way through them all.

'Grab her! She's robbed me blind!' Mr

Noble yelled.

No one moved. Or if they did it was to hold on to their own parcels more tightly. Faces and shops and stalls sped by as Pearl kept running. The four remaining parcels thudded against her ribs. She couldn't hold them much longer. One fell away. Then another. She hesitated. There wasn't time to stop. She wasn't even sure she could, for the icy pavement was smooth as glass beneath her feet.

Behind her came more shouts, not Mr Noble this time, but younger voices. A quick glance over her shoulder confirmed it: two men were giving chase. Pearl tried to go faster. Her feet spun on the snow. Then, lurching forward, she found a new burst of speed.

As the crowd closed around her, she tried to keep going, but the tide of people was too strong. Heart thumping, Pearl slowed to a brisk walk. As she glanced behind, she saw a mass of dark coats and hats bent against the snow. And right in the thick of it were two men, elbows sharp, pushing their way through. Pearl gritted her teeth.

On the right was a narrow alley where the buildings stood so close together they almost blocked out the sky. She nipped down it, and when she was sure no one had followed, stopped for a moment to catch her breath. A horrible sinking feeling came over her then. She realised what a foolish thing she'd done.

She'd only wanted to make Christmas special, to go home with armfuls of ingredients and make a pudding fit for a queen. But nicking stuff from Mr Noble was *not* the way to go about it. All she'd done was to make herself a thief.

Pearl straightened her shoulders. It wasn't too late to do the proper thing. Not if she went now and said sorry right away, and returned what packages she still had.

But as she turned to go back, two dark shapes blocked the passageway.

'Not so fast,' a man said.

Deep in her stomach, she felt a stab of fear.

'How's about you come quietly?' he said, inching towards her.

Pearl stepped backwards.

'I'm on my way to hand myself in,' she said. 'I don't need no escorting.'

The man and his companion came closer. She couldn't see either of their faces, but she could smell their stale tobacco breath.

'If you'll just let me by . . .'

As she tried to dodge past them, the first man seized her by the scruff.

'That ain't how it works. We take you back to Mr Noble – with what you nicked – and we gets a reward, see?'

Pearl lashed out with her feet. She felt her boot hit something hard.

'Arrgghhh!' the man cried, letting go of her to grab his shin. 'Get the parcels off her, Jack!'

From the shadows, the second man grabbed her arms. But Pearl wasn't going anywhere with these two. With a duck and a twist, she wrenched herself free.

'Oi! You little thiever! Get back here!'

Out on the open street, Pearl ran as fast as her legs would go. Behind her the thud of boots on cobbles filled her ears. She was heading in the wrong direction for Mr Noble's now, but she had to keep going.

Up ahead she saw the grey bulk of St Mark's church. Just before it was a tall white house where cats dozed in the windows. She knew this road, all right. She'd walked it with Agnes many times, always just to coo at the sleeping cats. The memory of it made her nose tingle.

There was no time for tears now, though. Or for cats. Before even reaching the white house, she ran left on to Devonshire Street. The road, busy with carriages and costermongers, was deep in grubby snow. Horses slipped on it. Cart wheels spun. Yet Pearl didn't dare slow down.

Up ahead on the right was another alleyway. If she'd remembered it correctly, it would take her back out on to the main street, not far from Mr Noble's shop. She'd go straight to him and apologise. She'd explain that her family was about to become rich. That Pa had gone to Bath today and would come home again with the most stunning news. It helped, thinking like this. It banished her doubts, and perhaps it would convince Mr Noble that she hadn't meant to steal, not really.

The men still followed. Pearl knew the

alley wasn't far now – twenty yards at most. But the men were shouting 'Stop! Thief!' so loudly that people began to take notice. On the pavement, a candle seller tried to block her path. Then a pie man stuck his foot out; as she jumped it another of her packages fell away.

At last Pearl reached the alley. Blindly, she swung right. Her legs were growing heavy. She felt a pain in her side. But as she slowed, a sickening sense of dread came over her. This alley looked different. What should've been the back gates of Devonshire Street's shops was instead a row of dingy houses. Up ahead was a brick wall. A dead end. Her heart thumped. It wasn't the right alley at all. Too late, she realised she was cornered.

The men's footsteps echoed behind her. There had to be a way out. Panicking, she noticed one house had its back door open, steam wafting from it like fog. The sharp smell of soap told her it was washday; already rows of laundry hung frozen stiff on the line.

Quick as anything, Pearl bobbed under a pair of long johns and slipped in through the open door. Inside, the house felt warm. Somewhere upstairs, a woman was singing a Christmas carol.

Pearl faltered. Half a meat pie sat temptingly on the table. By the stove was a chair draped in blankets. She suddenly felt very tired. Her stomach growled loudly as she remembered she'd not eaten breakfast.

It wouldn't hurt just to sit for a minute, she thought to herself, and why keep running, anyway? She might as well give herself up. Let those thugs march her back to Mr Noble. Besides, all she had left to make Christmas pudding with was . . . well, she wasn't actually sure. She glanced down at the one remaining package. It was damp and squished in her arms. She'd no idea what was inside, but it wouldn't make a pudding by itself.

That wasn't all.

Her shoulders felt chill of a sudden. Her wrists looked white and frail. No wonder. This morning she'd come out wrapped in a paisley shawl. Now, she realised in horror, it'd gone.

Desperate, she racked her brains. She'd been wearing it in the shop, hadn't she? It must've come off in the passage when the men tried to grab her.

Perhaps it was still there. The thought of it lying in a stinking alleyway made her eyes fill with tears. How the heck would she explain it to Ma?

Then, above her head, the ceiling creaked. Footsteps moved across it. She heard singing at the top of the stairs. Pearl held her breath.

Someone was coming down.

4

Festive Spirit

There had to be another way out, for Pearl couldn't leave the way she'd come in, not with those men still following. She pushed open the kitchen door. It led into a small, fireless parlour. There, straight ahead, was another door – a front door – with blue glass panels at the top. Pearl raced up to it. Tucking her last parcel under her arm, she grabbed the handle with both hands and twisted it. The door wouldn't budge. Behind her, one by one the stairs creaked. Any second she'd be discovered, here in a stranger's house. The police would be called. She'd be for it. Any second now . . .

With a sudden groan, the door swung open. Noise, snow, traffic, all flashed before her. There wasn't a pavement. She stepped right out into the street.

'Look out!' someone yelled.

Pearl froze. A carriage was coming straight towards her. She saw a blur of hooves. Heard a scream. The carriage slammed into her shoulder, her hip. The force of it knocked her sideways. She didn't feel pain, only the sense that her chest had been stamped on. And then she was falling backwards as if she'd never stop.

Yet, with a bone-jarring jolt, she did,

landing on a heap of snow on the other side of the road with her legs twisted beneath her. When she tried to get up, she couldn't move. Or breathe.

I've died, Pearl thought. *That's why I can't get my breath. That's why nothing hurts.*

Then her lungs eased and her breath came back. Every single part of her hurt, though her left ankle pained her the most.

'I didn't mean to hit her! She ran out in front of me!' a man was saying.

Three faces peered down at her.

'Thank heavens she's alive!' gasped a woman, who was starting to seem familiar.

'No doubt your screams brought her back from the brink, Mrs Lockwood,' said another man, who was wearing a dark blue jacket and matching hat.

Pearl blinked. *Oh crikey*, she thought. *It's Mrs Lockwood. And here I am sat on my backside again!* The person talking was a policeman. She had to hide her parcel. It was proof she was a thief. But the package lay just out of reach, its contents scattered across the snow in little yellow pieces.

Candied peel, Pearl thought, her eyes growing heavy. *What a waste.*

Someone shook her. 'Don't swoon again, miss.'

'I'm not swooning,' Pearl said. 'I'm fine.' But as she tried to stand, her ankle wouldn't hold her and she sank back into the snow.

Then, further off, came a shout. 'There she is!'

Dodging through the now stationary traffic, two men raced towards her. Pearl winced: so Mr Noble's men had caught up with her at last. It was over. She couldn't run any more.

Yet a few yards off the men stopped. Pulling down their caps and turning up their collars, they started backing away like they'd had a serious case of second thoughts.

Pearl frowned: what *were* they doing? Were they coming to get her or not?

Then she realised.

They'd spotted the policeman, and wouldn't come any closer. It made her feel safe and cross all at once. So much for *them* calling *her* a thiever! Perhaps they weren't even Mr Noble's men at all. Perhaps they'd just wanted to rob *her* blind. The idea made her shudder. She watched until the men were out of sight, to be sure they'd really gone.

Mrs Lockwood, it seemed, was also keen to be gone, but the policeman insisted on writing down exactly what had happened.

'The time of the accident was ten twenty-seven a.m.,' he said, consulting his pocket watch.

Mrs Lockwood tutted. 'Really, there's no need . . .'

'There's *every* need,' the policeman said,

and carried on writing.

The snow fell faster now. Pearl had grown very cold, her teeth chattering like mad things. She was beginning to worry about Ma too, who'd have got the stove hot and would be expecting her home to make the pudding.

At last the policeman put his notebook away.

'Is Mr Lockwood travelling with you, ma'am?' he asked.

'My husband is in Bath today,' Mrs Lockwood said.

Pearl shuffled into a sitting position: *Bath?* Perhaps Mr Lockwood would encounter Pa on the way, and they'd travel through the snow together. Wouldn't *that* be grand?

Yet more of a concern was how she'd get home, for she still couldn't stand up.

'Then you've room to take this poor girl to her destination,' said the policeman.

Mrs Lockwood glared at him. 'Really, officer, I hardly think that's necessary!'

'Under the circumstances, I think it is,' said the policeman. 'You'd not want to seem uncaring, would you? Not in such a public place?'

She glanced nervously at the busy street. People were staring, of course they were. Everyone knew the Lockwoods. They had a name. A reputation.

'Very well, we'll take the child home,' Mrs Lockwood said, with a smile that didn't reach her eyes.

'Excellent, Mrs Lockwood,' said the policeman. 'A little festive spirit goes a long way.'

She turned from him to address Pearl. 'Come along now. We need to make haste: this weather is worsening.'

Despite being certain she'd embarrassed Mrs Lockwood yet again, Pearl felt a quiver of excitement. She'd never ridden in a carriage before. But the fact was she *really couldn't* walk, so Cullen, the driver, heaved her upright then helped her into the carriage. The door closed with an expensive click.

Inside, two seats faced each other; she was in one, and Mrs Lockwood, under a fur coverlet, was in the other. The air was thick with the scent of lilies. Pearl supposed this was how ladies smelled. It made her feel slightly queasy.

Cullen whistled to his horses and with an almighty lurch the carriage moved off. Pearl, her back to the driver, had to grip onto her seat to stop herself sliding into Mrs Lockwood's lap. Even so, their knees bumped awkwardly.

'Sorry, ma'am,' Pearl muttered.

Mrs Lockwood didn't answer. She sat bolt upright, hands crossed over the package she'd purchased in Mr Noble's shop.

Purchased, not thieved, Pearl thought with a pang of guilt. But all that was about to change, she reminded herself, just as soon as Pa came home from Bath.

Outside the carriage window, the snow fell so thickly it was almost a fog. Horses went by, their rumps turned powdery white. What few people still walked the pavements hurried along with their heads down. The carriage seemed to slow, then turn, then slow again. Cullen shouted. The horses whinnied. They came to a complete stop.

Mrs Lockwood tapped on the carriage roof. 'Whatever's happening?'

The vehicle rocked. With a thud Cullen jumped down, then appeared at the window, plastered in snow.

'Sorry, ma'am,' he said. 'They're saying Heather Lane is impassable. Two carts have just gone over from trying.'

Pearl sat forward. Heather Lane was *her* lane, where she lived. There was no other way to get home. And what of Pa, who'd later be coming all the way from Bath? He'd never make it back in this weather. Any excitement she'd felt started to ebb rather quickly away.

Mrs Lockwood let out an enormous huff. 'This is ridiculous, Cullen. Can't you . . . well . . . *do* something?'

'Can't stop it snowing, ma'am,' he said.

'Then how are we to get this child home?' She glared at Pearl in a way that seemed to say this was all *her* fault.

Pearl's spirits sank lower. So much for her family's luck changing: this was meant to be a proper Christmas. And yet it was fast becoming the worst of days. All because of some poxy letter from some la-di-da uncle she'd never even met.

'I've an idea, ma'am,' Cullen said.

'What is it?' Mrs Lockwood snapped.

'The way we've just come is still passable. If we turn round now, we'll reach the Manor within half an hour.'

As Mrs Lockwood mulled it over, Pearl felt her own heart plummet. Flintfield Manor was the Lockwood family home. It was a sprawling house with smart lawns and vast windows. Not that Pearl had been there, but she'd heard about it plenty from Pa. Any other time she'd have relished a gander at the place. Now, though, it made her wring her hands in agitation.

'I can't go with you, ma'am,' she said.

'It's only until the snow passes,' said Mrs Lockwood. 'Don't make a fuss.'

But Ma would be expecting her back by now; she was probably anxious already. The walk to Mr Noble's never took *this* long, and since Agnes died, her ma was prone to worry. Pearl could picture her checking at the windows and pacing up and down. It made her squirm uncomfortably.

Yet, sure enough, the carriage turned and set off towards the Manor. They travelled faster, as if they were racing against the weather. Snowflakes whipped past the windows. Bitter air breathed under the door, turning Pearl's toes to ice. Colder still was the unease settling inside her. She shut her eyes; it didn't help. All she wanted was to go home.

When she looked up, Mrs Lockwood was watching her.

'You appear unwell, child,' she said.

'No, ma'am,' she said, feeling her chin tremble like it did when she was about to cry.

Really she should be grateful. Mrs Lockwood could've left her by the roadside. Instead she was offering her shelter from the snow. If Pearl forgot that Ma was at home waiting . . . if she forgot about Pa walking to Bath . . . if she forgot it was Christmas Eve, then really it was a kindness.

But that only made the tears come, and the stupid things rolled down her face, splashing on to her dress front.

'Oh dear,' said Mrs Lockwood, tucking the still-warm fur coverlet around her legs before she could object.

Goodness! More festive spirit! Pearl thought, staring at it in amazement.

'It won't bite,' Mrs Lockwood said, with a smile. 'Those mink died years ago.'

Pearl wiped her face dry. 'Thank you, ma'am, you're very kind.'

'Oh, don't thank me,' said Mrs Lockwood, making a great show of huddling into her coat. 'I simply don't want you dying of cold in my carriage. Imagine how *that* would look.'

Which didn't seem quite so festive after all.

5

Sugared Plums

Flintfield Manor was an extremely tall house. Craning her neck at the carriage window, Pearl counted five floors, including attics and the basement. The house was made of fox-red bricks, with sills and front steps in the same cream-coloured stone. It all looked very neat and very new. Almost like a picture of a home, rather than a real one, Pearl thought.

She'd never been this close to a rich person's house, and wondered if Silas Granger – *Uncle* Silas, as was – had lived in a house like Flintfield. *Perhaps that was what he'd left them in his will!* It was an exciting, thrilling thought. And yet, somehow, she couldn't imagine quite how it would feel.

Once Cullen had helped Mrs Lockwood inside, he drove round to a stable yard. Rows of well-bred horses' heads appeared over the doors to greet them.

'Am I to stay in the stables?' Pearl asked, as Cullen opened the carriage door.

He laughed. But she wasn't being funny; a bed of warm straw would do until morning.

'You and these plums are going to the kitchens,' said Cullen.

He picked up the package from Mr Noble's shop that Mrs Lockwood's had left on her seat, and in one quick swoop heaved Pearl over his shoulder. Half of Pearl's blood rushed to her head. The rest went to her ankle, making it throb like a sting.

Cullen followed a cinder path right up to the back door. On the step, he kicked the snow off his boots.

'Put me down!' Pearl protested.

Cullen chuckled. 'It's a fair walk to the kitchens, miss.'

It was too. Pearl lost count of the passages, the doors, the steps. At last they reached the kitchens.

'Those boots of yours better be clean!' someone called.

'Could eat your supper off them, Mrs D,' Cullen replied, handing over Mrs Lockwood's package and dropping Pearl on a stool beside the range.

Slowly, the room righted itself. Pearl

pushed her hair from her eyes and gasped. Everywhere she looked was white marble – cupboard tops, tabletops, boards for working pastry, even the floor at her feet. It was like being outside in the snow still, only a hundred times warmer.

As for food, there was enough here to feed a whole village. There were meat pies and fruit pies, little egg tarts on a cooling rack. Scrubbed vegetables lay in heaps, beef roasted on the range. *This was a Christmas feast*, Pearl thought, mouth watering. It made her pudding plans look shabby indeed.

Up on a shelf she spotted a row of muslin-wrapped basins: proper *Christmas puddings*, she thought, counting at least ten. She pictured all the currants and mixed peel and sugar gone into them, and it made her head spin.

When Pa came back rich they'd eat like this, she told herself. *Everything would be just grand.*

Only this time it didn't help. Not when Ma was at home fretting, and she was stuck here, as much use to anyone as a bucket with a hole in it.

Cullen, meanwhile, was speaking to the woman he'd addressed as 'Mrs D', who was too busy to stay still.

'What am I meant to do with her?' she said, pointing her wooden spoon at Pearl.

'Keep her warm and out of the way. She's hurt her ankle, see?'

The woman glared at Pearl's foot. 'But I've food to prepare for tomorrow. If it's not fit for a king it'll be *my* guts for garters.'

'Sorry, Mrs Davey. 'Tis orders.'

'Aye. It's been nothing but *orders* today. Been in a right fluster since Mr Lockwood took off this morning, she has. And as for those *brattish girls* . . . well!'

The girls in question, Pearl guessed,

were Mrs Lockwood's daughters: Olivia, Clementina and Annabel. Sometimes she saw them about town in the carriage. On one warm day with the windows down, she'd heard them too, saying the most awful, spiteful things to each other. Such pretty girls they'd looked – as delicate as fine china. Yet what came from their mouths that day would've shocked a street sweeper! Pearl hadn't forgotten it, even now.

Once Mrs Davey had shooed Cullen from her kitchen, she summoned one of the kitchen maids to tend to Pearl.

'Sit her somewhere else, Martha, will you?' she said. 'I don't mind where – just keep her out of our way.'

Pearl felt her colour rise. She didn't want to be a nuisance. As she stood up, though, her ankle gave. Martha caught her by the arm as she swayed.

'Let's have a look at that, shall we?' she said.

The kitchen maid wasn't much older than Pearl, yet she had a bossy, bubbly way that made her seem more in charge than she was. After sitting her at the table in a sturdy chair, she eased Pearl's boot off. Except for an egg-sized lump at her ankle, it didn't look too bad.

'Wriggle them toes,' said Martha.

Pearl did as she was told.

'Good. Now your ankle.'

She winced. It hurt. But the movement soon freed it up.

'Well, it don't seem broken,' said Martha, sitting back on her heels.

Pearl smiled shyly; Martha smiled back.

'Those carrots scrubbed yet?' Mrs Davey called over.

Martha sprang to her feet. 'Nearly, Mrs D!'

'Get a shift on, then. You've still to do the sugared plums.'

Martha groaned.

'I'll do them, if you like,' said Pearl, for she wanted to help if she could.

'Would you? Sets my teeth on edge, all that sugar.'

First Martha insisted Pearl prop up her ankle on a box. Mrs Davey was not amused.

'We aren't here to spoil *you* rotten,' she said to Pearl. 'Enough of that goes on upstairs.'

Pearl lowered her foot guiltily.

'I ain't spoiling her, Mrs D. She's helping with the plums,' Martha said.

Once Mrs Davey wasn't looking, she slid the box back in place with her toe. Pearl fought down a smile.

'Right, then,' Martha said, unwrapping Mrs Lockwood's package. Inside were two jars crammed with dark purple fruit. The labels said 'Noble's Finest Preserved Plums' in swirly gold writing. 'Do both jars.

Miss Clementina and Miss Olivia have got a proper sweet tooth.'

'So they must have!' Pearl gasped.

One Christmas, they'd made half a dozen sugared plums. Ma and Agnes nibbled theirs slowly, but she'd eaten hers all in one go. She remembered how the syrup had coated her teeth. It had made her feel royally sick.

Now, though, it helped to have a job to do. It kept her mind off poor Ma. Pearl folded back her sleeves, and with a tray of sugar before her, she rolled plum after sticky plum in it till the crust was thick. Then she laid them carefully on a baking sheet. They'd be warmed above the range just till the sugar softened. Then she'd roll them all over again.

By the time she'd finished there were forty-five sugared plums. They did look, Pearl admitted, quite tasty. No doubt they'd be taken upstairs in a dainty glass dish to be served with port wine before a fire.

'Them girls'll make short work of those,' said Martha, coming over to admire Pearl's handiwork.

'They'll eat *all* of them?'

'I'd put a shilling on it. They'll fight over the last one and all.'

'Blimey,' said Pearl.

She'd never argued much with Agnes. And definitely not over something as stupid as a plum.

6

The White Room

The kitchen staff worked late into the evening. There were cakes to be glazed, birds to be plucked. The place was a whirl of activity. Outside, the snow fell thick as goose feathers, and with each flake Pearl knew her chances of getting home tonight grew slimmer. By now Ma would be beside herself with worry. And as for Pa, who could guess where he was? This really was the very worst Christmas Eve she'd ever had.

When at bedtime Mr Lockwood still hadn't returned from Bath, it was decided to leave the front door unlocked.

'Hope he ain't in a ditch somewhere,' said Martha with a shudder.

Pearl, who'd been thinking the same about Pa, dearly wished she'd shut up.

'That's enough, Martha,' Mrs Davey said. 'Now, I'm locking the kitchens. We don't want a thief walking in and helping himself. That meat alone is worth a fortune.'

Thief.

Just the word made Pearl hot and prickly. Mrs Davey couldn't possibly know what had happened at Mr Noble's, *could she*? She didn't see how. But it made her feel guilty again, all the same.

'So where's Pearl to sleep?' said Martha.

'I already share with Nettie, who snores more than any maid I've ever met. I can't be doing with someone else.'

'I don't snore,' said Pearl, for this was one flaw she knew she didn't have.

'There's that spare bed in the attics,' said Mrs Davey.

Martha pulled a face. 'You can't put her in the white room!'

'Oh, stop your nonsense!' Mrs Davey snapped.

'*I* wouldn't sleep in there,' Martha said. 'Not after last time.'

'What happened?' Pearl couldn't resist asking.

Martha's eyes went very wide. 'Well,' she said, pausing dramatically, 'I had the queerest, most awful dreams. And I felt, somehow, like something was making me look outside through the window, like I had no choice . . .

I can't explain it . . .'

'Don't, then,' Mrs Davey cut in. 'Now get yourselves to bed. We've an early start in the morning.'

There was no need for candles. Martha led the way up a wooden staircase that was lit by gas jets on the walls. She climbed quickly, and though Pearl tried to keep up, her ankle was weak so she had to stop every few steps to rest. By the time she'd reached the first landing, Martha was waiting. Or not waiting, exactly, for just off the staircase was a door, and Martha's ear was pressed against it.

'Told you them plums'd start a row!' she grinned, beckoning for Pearl to join her.

The door was slightly ajar.

'Come closer!' Martha hissed.

Pearl took a couple more steps. The air wafting through the door felt warm against her cheek. With it came voices. Just feet away, on the other side, were the Lockwoods, in what she guessed must be their parlour. She leaned closer still.

'Tell her, Mama. She *shan't* have more sugared plums than me!'

'Oh, Olivia, do stop whining.' This was Mrs Lockwood herself.

'But she's already had twenty-five. I've counted.'

'I'm only saving your figure, sister dearest,' said another voice. 'You've clearly had to be laced in tightly this evening.'

'Have not!'

'Have so! Look how red your face is!'

Martha stifled a giggle, then moved aside for Pearl. 'Have a peep through the gap! Those girls look a right sorry sight!'

Pearl hesitated. She was dying for a glimpse of the Lockwood sisters, but she really didn't fancy getting caught. She'd caused enough trouble for one day.

'Hadn't we better go up?' she said. 'I think I hear Mrs Davey coming.'

She wasn't. But Martha moved on.

The attics ran right across the top of the house. Doors fanned off a long, narrow corridor – not fancy doors like downstairs, but plain ones like in Pearl's own bed chamber at home.

Martha nodded to her left. 'Your room's that way. First one you get to. Rather you than me,' she added with a shudder.

Yet the room she was to sleep in looked normal enough. It was low-ceilinged and bare, apart from an iron bed, at the foot of which was a rolled-up blanket and pillow. Yawning, Pearl made up her bed, then unlaced her boots, easing her sore ankle out gently. The climb up all those stairs had left her limp as a dishrag. Never mind Martha's daft stories about looking out of the window – she reckoned she'd sleep like the dead.

Sure enough, she soon drifted off. But it was an uneasy, fretful sleep that had her twisting and turning and sweating through her clothes. She dreamed of Ma shovelling snow off the path, and of Agnes crying and begging her to leave it just where it was. And she – Pearl – watched from her bedroom window, but when she tried calling and banging on the glass, no one heard her.

With a gasp, Pearl's eyes flew open. She had no idea where she was. It seemed she was in a strange bed beneath a window with no curtains. Bright squares of moonlight fell on to the blanket. And the room itself, with its painted floor and distempered walls, seemed to give off a bluish glow. Everything was silent and still, yet her heart was beating as loud as thunder. Then it came back to her where she was.

She sat up. The hairs on her neck prickled.

Instinct made her glance upwards. The window was iced over. There was nothing to see. And yet she felt suddenly certain that someone was outside in the snow; she had to see who.

Unsteadily, she stood on the bed and reached up. The catch was stiff, but with a heave and a clunk the window opened like a hatch. She poked her head out into the bitter night air.

'Hullo?' she called. 'Who's there?'

No one replied.

Pearl wriggled through the window a bit more. Now she saw how the snow-covered rooftops sloped away in all directions, each with little windows just like hers. And where the roofs ended, gutters and leadwork

gleamed in the moonlight. From up here the house looked vast, almost magical. It was like gazing out over a dreamworld.

So this was how rich people lived, she realised. Very soon, if Uncle Silas's will proved right, she might be living this way herself. Squeezing her eyes tight shut, Pearl tried to imagine it: the carriages, the sugared plums, the rustling silk dresses. But all she could picture was Agnes's paisley shawl abandoned somewhere in a gutter. It made her feel slightly ill.

Giving up, Pearl opened her eyes. It had started to snow again. Already the rooftops, the grass, the driveway looked whiter and smoother than before.

There was definitely no one out here. It was Martha's stupid story that had turned her head, that was all. Shivering with cold, she began to ease herself back through the window.

Suddenly, she went still.

What was that, standing on the path to the stables?

Pearl looked harder. Her heart began to boom.

There were no footprints, no obvious signs of disturbance. And yet a person-sized shape stood upright in the snow. Pearl breathed in sharp. She rubbed her eyes. There was no mistaking the tilt of its head, looking straight at her attic window. No mistaking either the weight in Pearl's chest.

'Agnes?' she called. 'Is that you?'

Pearl pressed her eyes with the heels of her hands. She must still be asleep. This had to be part of her dream. Or maybe Martha was right, that this *was* a queer room. Whatever the truth of it, Pearl knew she couldn't look away.

The snow danced thickly before her. With

her face full of tears and wind-whipped hair, it was hard to see anything at all.

'Agnes!' she cried. 'Agnes!'

Frantic, Pearl leaned outwards, the window ledge digging into her ribs.

'Agnes! Don't go! Don't leave me!'

A sudden gust of wind lifted the hair from her eyes. And in that moment she saw.

The path was clear.

She'd imagined it, hadn't she?

There was no snow sister. No Agnes. It was time she realised it properly. Her sister had gone. Nor would she ever see her again.

❦ 7 ❧

A Bequest

S he must have fallen asleep eventually, because when Pearl opened her eyes the window above her framed the most perfect blue sky. She blinked. From deep within the house came the sounds of doors shutting, maids calling, footsteps going up and down stairs.

It was Christmas morning. Today was

meant to be special – the Granger family's first proper Christmas in years. Yet her poor ma probably hadn't slept a wink for worrying. And here she was, miles from home and still in bed!

Throwing back the covers, Pearl stood shakily on her feet. Her injured ankle held. Once she'd got her boots on it felt stronger still, strong enough, she hoped, to get her home.

Something else lingered in her mind like the tail end of a dream. Climbing up on the bed, she pushed open the window.

Outside, everything was dazzling white. It hurt her eyes just to look. That place on the path where last night she thought she'd seen her snow sister was smooth, untouched snow. She definitely *had* imagined it, hadn't she? Yet the pain of missing Agnes still felt very real.

A sharp knock at the door and Martha's face appeared round it, a sprig of holly in her cap. Hastily, Pearl got off the bed.

'Good sleep, was it?' Martha grinned. 'No strange goings-on?'

'Not that I noticed,' said Pearl, though she couldn't meet Martha's eye.

'Good. Can't stop. We're serving breakfast.' And she disappeared off down the stairs.

Pearl followed. Out in the stairwell, she smelled bacon and toasted bread. The shadows deep inside her began to lift. It was Christmas Day. Once she got home, who knew what great news Pa might bring from Bath. No, she decided, today she'd try her very hardest not to be sad.

On the first-floor landing she found Martha, hands full of steaming dishes, struggling to open the door into the Lockwoods' parlour. Behind her, Nettie carried muffins and bread. Pearl hovered on the staircase for them to pass.

'Don't drop it!' Nettie warned, as Martha's load slid sideways. 'Mr Lockwood won't like it if his haddock spoils.'

'He'd be happy eating carpet this morning,' Martha laughed.

Pearl's heart did a skip. 'He made it back, then?' she asked. For surely if the Bath road was clear, Pa would have got home as well.

Martha glanced her way. 'Aye, and full of good news he is too.'

'Oh, get a move on, Martha, and open that door!' Nettie scolded.

'I'll do it.' Ducking between them, Pearl pushed the door.

Martha and Nettie bustled through without a backwards glance. Pearl hesitated. She ought to shut the door. Be on her way. But while the clinking of cutlery on china came from the room next door, *this* room – the parlour – was empty. A quick peep wouldn't hurt.

Pearl tiptoed inside. In an alcove by the fire was a Christmas tree as tall as the ceiling. So many glittery things hung off it, the branches fairly sagged. Yet the rest of the room didn't seem much like a parlour at all. The arched stone fireplace looked hundreds of years old. Tapestries showing dogs chasing deer hung from the walls. Even the furniture looked heavy and dark. The whole effect was of a vast, ancient room. Almost, she supposed, like a castle.

'Looks old, dunnit? But it's all brand new, bought from a fancy shop in London,' whispered Martha at her shoulder.

Pearl jumped. 'Sorry . . . I . . . I was just on my way.'

'Stay there a minute, would you? I need your help with the door. I'm coming back up with another tray.'

So Pearl waited, though by now she was fidgety to be gone. The parlour had hardly been worth snooping at after all. Fancy or not, it didn't look very homely. It was too bleak and hard.

Martha returned carrying a tray of tall glasses and a wine bottle so cold it seemed to be sweating.

'Champagne for breakfast!' she grinned, as Pearl held open the door. 'They're celebrating more than Christmas this morning!'

'Oh?'

Martha dropped her voice. 'Mr Lockwood's only gone and come home from Bath *twice* as rich as when he went!'

Pearl frowned. 'How?'

'Some person's left him their fortune.'

Then Nettie appeared in search of the champagne. 'Martha! No time for chat! Quickly now!'

Pulling a face, Martha followed her with the tray.

Funny that Mr Lockwood had been to Bath, Pearl thought. Funny too that he'd been left something in a will, though she supposed plenty of rich people died in Bath.

The door to the adjoining room stood open, the voices coming through sounding loud and jovial.

'So, my dear, will you choose your present? Is it to be diamonds?' The speaker was a man – Mr Lockwood, she guessed.

'Oh, Charles! I couldn't possibly!' Mrs Lockwood giggled.

'Choose, Mama, oh do!' said a young voice Pearl recognised from yesterday. 'A necklace and matching earrings will be divine! And we can wear them too!'

'*You?* In diamonds?' said another girl. 'I hardly *think* so, Olivia.'

'Girls, don't be beastly!' Mrs Lockwood said.

'Well, Clementina, at least I don't have the table manners of a pig.'

Knives clattered on to plates. Someone said, 'Ouch!'

'Let go of her, you silly creature!' Mrs Lockwood cried, then in happier tones to her husband, 'Tell us, dear, exactly *how* much were you left?'

Mr Lockwood coughed. 'In the region of thirty thousand pounds, I do believe.'

There were squeals of delight. Gasps of shock.

Pearl clapped her hand over her mouth.

Thirty thousand pounds!

It was a heck of a lot of money. A fortune, no less. Enough for a lifetime of credit at Mr Noble's shop. Enough to buy . . . She stopped. She'd no idea what the Lockwoods might buy, since they hardly wanted for much. They were already the richest people she knew.

And thanks to Uncle Silas her family might soon be rich too, though what would *they* do with an amount like £30,000, she wondered? To think in a few hours' time it could be *her* family sat around *their* table, having a conversation just like this! It felt utterly bizarre.

The champagne cork popped, jolting Pearl from her thoughts. One of the daughters giggled. A chair was pushed back. The floorboards creaked. Then Mr Lockwood said, 'I propose a toast.'

More chairs scraped the floor. Skirts rustled as Mrs Lockwood and her daughters got to their feet.

'To Silas Granger, for his fortune!'

'To Silas Granger!' came the reply.

Pearl's hand, still covering her mouth,

smothered her cry.

Silas Granger? *Uncle* Silas?

This must be a mistake! It couldn't be true! Uncle Silas left his money to Pa, not to the Lockwoods, who had more than enough of it already!

But as the family sat down again and Mr Lockwood talked on, it was clear there was no mistake.

'I owe much to Silas Granger. He was, to me, a mentor. We worked together on the Darlington railway – buying and selling land, winning over the locals. He'd stop at nothing, that man. His ambitions were immense.'

'More than yours, Papa?' said Olivia.

'Perhaps. Some thought him ruthless. He married late but certainly never spent any time with his family – he had a brother and a daughter; his wife died before him. He put them all aside to make his fortune.'

'Why did he leave you his money, not his family?'

'Oh Olivia, stop being nosy,' said a girl's voice she'd not yet heard; Annabel, clearly.

'Yes, Olivia, do stop it!' added Clementina.

As Mr Lockwood cleared his throat, the girls fell silent.

'I believe Silas Granger saw me as the son he never had,' he said. 'He taught me all I know, my dears. He helped make me – make *us* – the fine family we are today!'

The trembling grew in Pearl's stomach. So this was the truth of it: there was no fortune for her family, after all. The lawyer's letter had said that her father was the main beneficiary, but it must have been wrong. She didn't know if what she felt was shock or relief. All she knew was she had to get home.

8

Comfort and Joy

'Blimey, you look like the cat's left-offs!' Martha said, as they met on the stairs.

'Got to dash!' Pearl said, rushing by. 'Ta for everything!'

At the bottom of the stairs, she went past the kitchens, up steps, down steps and finally out of the back door. In the yard, Cullen was brushing straw from a horse's tail.

'Merry Christmas, miss!' he called.

She waved. 'And to you!'

Walking as briskly as her ankle would allow, Pearl went up the driveway. The snow here was scored by fresh hoof prints. She pictured Mr Lockwood crouched low over the reins, hurrying his horse homewards because he couldn't wait to share his news. Poor Pa would have no such tidings, she realised, and felt disappointment unfurl inside her. It would've been better if Uncle Silas had left them *something*. This way felt quite unfair.

Already the Lockwoods had a handsome house and kitchens groaning with food. Now they had £30,000 more. All thanks to Silas Granger, who'd chosen a man with whom he'd once built a railway over his own brother.

No, it wasn't right.

Angry now, Pearl kicked the snow. She was

tired and hungry. Her ankle, though stronger, had started to throb. Yet what niggled her most were those Lockwood sisters, whose whinging and squabbling still rang in her ears. She and Agnes never spoke like that. If they argued, they'd always laugh it off again.

Goodness, how she wanted to shake those Lockwood girls. Didn't they *realise* what they had?

Not the £30,000 or their rustling silk dresses and certainly not those sugared plums.

What they had was *each other*.

She'd give anything to have a sister sat across from her at breakfast. Here were the Lockwood girls with *two* sisters apiece! And she'd not heard a civil word pass between them.

Yet despite herself, Pearl saw it was a glorious morning. The sun on her cheek felt almost warm. And when she did finally reach

Heather Lane, her mood began to lift. For a trail of footprints led right up to her gate, and that meant Pa was home.

She stopped. There were *two* people's footprints here. Her stomach did a somersault. Mr Noble's thugs must've come looking for her. And once Ma knew she was a thief, well, that was one telling-off she'd never escape.

Taking a big breath, she opened the gate. There, with her two coal eyes and a turnip for a nose, was her snow sister. Today, in the sunlight, she didn't seem quite so magical. In fact, she looked lumpy and rather grey.

On the front step, Pearl put her shoulder to the wood, for the door was inclined to stick. Then, all too fast, the door swung open. Still clinging to the handle, Pearl lurched inside and found herself face to face with a girl she'd never seen before.

'Who . . . *what?*'

Before the girl could answer, Ma rushed to the doorway.

'There you are!' she cried, flinging her arms around Pearl. She smelled deliciously of baking. Shutting the door, Ma glanced at her daughter's feet. 'Which ankle was it, then?'

Pearl frowned. 'How d'you know about that? Where's Pa? And who's this?' She gestured to the girl, who was dressed all in black and fidgeted nervously with her hands – fine white hands they were too, Pearl noticed.

'One thing at a time,' said Ma, tucking a curl behind Pearl's ear. She was smiling, which was even more confusing. Had Mr Noble's men been, or not? Hadn't her ma been worried about her? She'd expected a few harsh words, at least.

'Yesterday, when you'd been gone a fair while, I came looking for you at Mr Noble's,' Ma said.

'Oh.' Pearl's heart sank. 'He told you?'

Ma pursed her lips, suddenly serious. 'He did. And that weren't right of you, Pearl. No girl of mine is a thief. Got that?'

Pearl nodded. She felt awful, doubly so for being told off in front of a stranger.

'But,' Ma said, 'he told me you'd been hurt, and that Mrs Lockwood took you in because of the snow. His men who'd tried to nab you brought back your shawl.'

'Agnes's shawl! Is it found?'

'It is.'

Pearl closed her eyes in relief. Perhaps the men weren't so thuggish after all.

'Mr Noble's keeping it for now, until we settle our account.'

Her eyes opened again. Thinking of the Lockwoods' fortune, she knew this wouldn't be any time soon.

Then the girl in the black dress made a

little noise in her throat.

'I'm sorry,' Pearl said, turning to her. 'But who *are* you? And where's my pa?'

As if in answer, Pa appeared from the direction of the cellar door, coal buckets in each hand.

'She's back!' he grinned.

Dropping his buckets, he put an arm round Pearl's shoulders and kissed the top of her head. For a man who'd been done out of £30,000, he seemed in surprisingly good spirits.

'Met your cousin, have you?' he said, nodding at the strange girl.

Pearl stared, aghast. 'My *cousin*?'

Now, for the first time, she really looked at the girl. She was about Pearl's age, though taller. The black dress meant she was in mourning. Of course she was, Pearl realised; the poor thing had just lost her pa. It was a well-cut frock that fell right to the floor, not like Pearl's, which even with the hems down ended short of her ankles.

The girl stepped forward, hand outstretched.

'I'm Joy,' she said.

Pearl kept staring. Where she had freckles, Joy's skin was as smooth as snow. Yet it was a sad face, very pinched and pale, and so unlike her lovely name.

'I'm Pearl,' she said, shaking Joy's hand.

She still didn't quite follow. So Joy was Uncle Silas's daughter. But why was she here, with them?

She glanced at Pa. Were those *tears* in his eyes?

'Tell us, then,' she said to him.

Pa sniffed. 'Well, see, Silas and me, we had our differences. He chose a life of business, I chose my family – you lot, that is. But what he

learned in the end, it seems, was that money distracted him from what really mattered. So he left his fortune to a man who has this lesson still to learn.'

'Mr Lockwood,' Pearl said.

Her pa nodded. 'Silas named me as the main beneficiary in his will but he didn't want all that money to turn our heads. What he left us was far greater than any fortune. He gave us his most precious thing.'

The way he looked at Joy made Pearl's eyes well up. She was beginning to understand.

'He knew we were a good family and what we'd suffered losing Agnes,' Pa said. 'And that no fortune would bring her back.'

Pearl bit down on her lip to stop it quivering. Last night at the window, hadn't she felt this too? The thought of being rich had been exciting in its way, yet no amount of silk dresses would replace her dear sister.

She pictured the Lockwoods bickering over breakfast this morning. Having money hadn't made them happy.

But she'd hoped at least not to go hungry any more. Now, though, they had another mouth to feed, and that meant more hard times, surely? It was difficult to believe Uncle Silas wanted *that* for his daughter.

Yet Pa didn't seem troubled; if anything he looked happier than she'd seen him in ages. He'd taken a seat by what was now a very warm stove. Ma sat beside him.

'So we're still poor, then?' Pearl said.

'Not completely,' said Pa. 'Your uncle left us his wife's jewellery. It's not much: a few rings, some pearls, a pretty brooch. She wasn't one for show, apparently. His instructions were to sell what was needed to help us bring up Joy – and you, Pearl.'

'Enough to put food in your bellies and

good clothes on your backs,' added Ma.

Turning to her cousin, Pearl began to feel a sort of glow. Maybe this was it: their luck was changing. Certainly this was fast becoming a wonderful Christmas. Joy's face softened into a smile as if she thought so too. Her eyes were grey, just like Agnes's. It was only a fleeting resemblance, but it was there, and it stirred something deep in Pearl's chest.

Through the window, she glimpsed her snow sister. Without Agnes's shawl it really was just a big, dirty lump of ice. Maybe it always had been. It was no good willing it to be something else. A shape in the snow would never replace her sister. Nor would a cousin, Pearl realised, because having a cousin was a wonderful thing all of its own.

And they were more than ready to welcome Joy into their lives.

If you enjoyed reading *The Snow Sister*,
read more by Emma Carroll . . .

'Like Michael Morpurgo
and Philip Pullman, Carroll . . .
knows she can keep her listeners
in thrall.' *Telegraph*

'A gripping adventure.'

Guardian

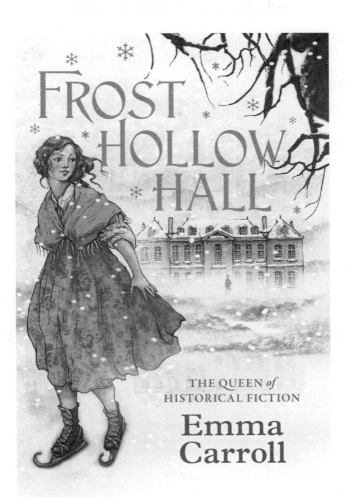

THE QUEEN *of*
HISTORICAL FICTION

Emma
Carroll

'For fans of Eva Ibbotson.'

WeLoveThisBook

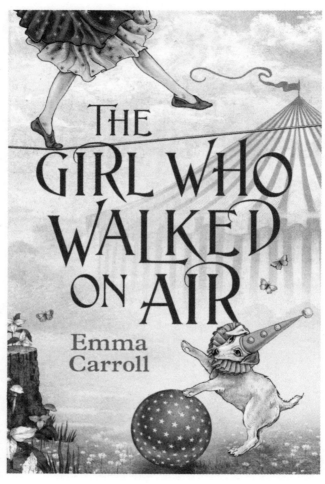

THE
GIRL WHO
WALKED
ON AIR

Emma
Carroll

Nominated –
CILIP Carnegie Medal

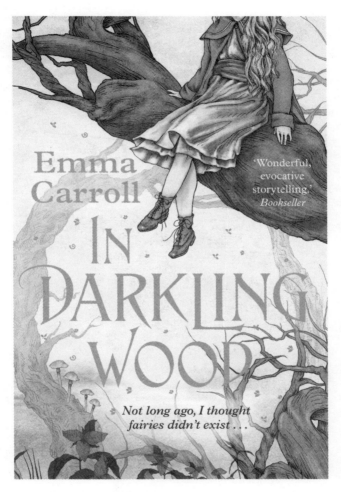

Emma
Carroll

In
Darkling
Wood

'Wonderful,
evocative
storytelling.'
Bookseller

*Not long ago, I thought
fairies didn't exist . . .*

'Absorbing, sensitive and
genuinely magical.'

Independent

'A deliciously gothic thriller
. . . her best yet.'

Bookseller